For the Bitter.

May you cease cannibalizing beloved carcasses in the roads behind and taste the sweeter meat of learned dishes on the trek ahead.

FLATLINE
COMICS
ROADKILL
PROPERTY
SHAWN
HARBIN

ROADKILL Du Jour

writer	**Kevin LaPorte** @kevinlaporte
artist	**Shawn Harbin**
colorist ch. 1-2, pp. 51-59	**Laura Guzzo** @lauraguzzoart
colorist pp. 58-70, ch. 4	**Yuan Cakra** @yuancakra
cover art	**Rando Dixon** @randodixonart
cover colors	**K. Michael Russell** @kmichaelrussell
chapter plates	**Amanda Rachels** @amandarachels

ROADKILL DU JOUR presented by INVERSE PRESS - 11101 Rachels Lane, Foley, AL 36535.

INVERSE

http://inversepress.com

facebook.com/flatlinecomics
Twitter: @inversepress
Instagram: @flatline_comics

"EMPTINESS KILL A MAN."

"OLE' EMPTINESS, IT A HOLE CUT OUTTA FAMILY LONG GONE.

"MERCY, I MISS'EM."

"BUT I JUS' RIDE ON WITHOUT'EM AN' TRY TA LIVE.

"I LIVED FO' ROADKILL THEN."

"AN' I LIVE ON ROADKILL NOW."

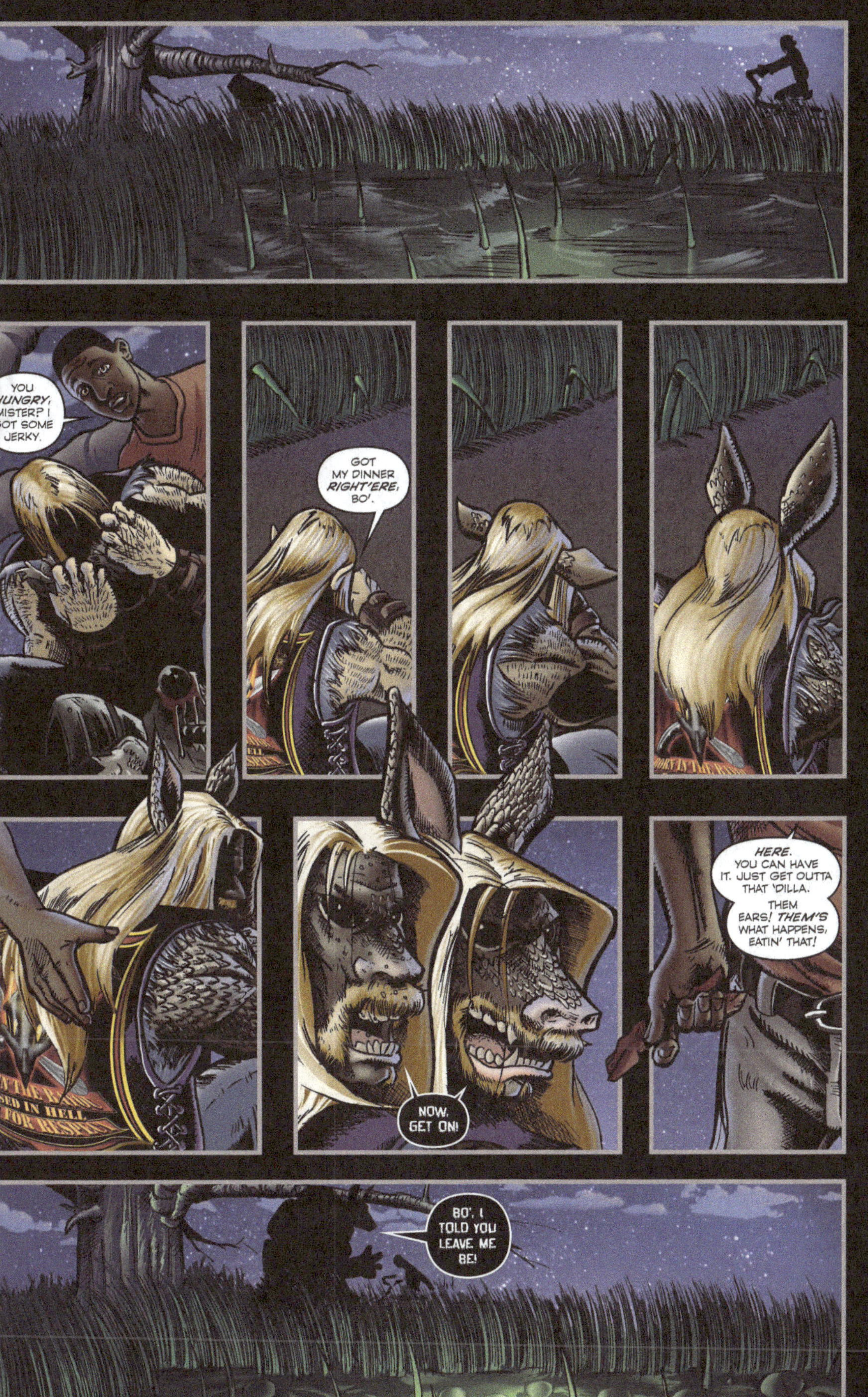

YOU HUNGRY, MISTER? I GOT SOME JERKY.
GOT MY DINNER RIGHT'ERE, BO'.
HERE. YOU CAN HAVE IT. JUST GET OUTTA THAT 'DILLA.
THEM EARS! THEM'S WHAT HAPPENS, EATIN' THAT!
NOW, GET ON!
BO', I TOLD YOU LEAVE ME BE!

SORRY, MISTER.
RUNNIN' FROM MY OLE MAN'S PLACE, JERKY'S ALL I COULD STEAL IN A HURRY.
HOLLER IF YO' MIND CHANGES. I'M HENNIE. HENNIE HILLIARD.
AIN'T NO MAN OUGHTTA EAT LIKE--
DUJOUR!
'NESSA?

THEY STUCK ME IN-BETWEEN, BABY!
WON'T LET LOOSE'A ME!
PUSH ME OR PULL ME!
VANESSA!

BUT DON'T LEAVE ME IN-BETWEEN!

I'M COMIN', SUGAR!
COME BACK!
IT'S JUS' AN OLE SPOOK-LIGHT!
CURFEW

HEY, MISTER!
COME OUT! DON'T FOLLA THAT THANG!
THERE YOU WENT!
AIN'T LOSIN' YOU THIS TIME! NOT AGAIN!
PLEASE. DUJUH--
VANESSA! DONE 'SCAPED ME AGAIN!
SORRY, BABY...

EATER!
WE SMELL OUR SUPPER, EATER!
THAT SAVORY DEATH CALLS US.
SALA-MAN--

--TELL ME WHERE MY 'NESSA WENT!
--'CUZ YOU AIN'T HER!
RAAWWWR!
PERHAPS WE ATE HER, EATER! LIKE WE EAT THE DEAD SPIRIT THAT POWERS YOU!

FEED US!
AND FEED US AGAIN!
GET OFF HIM, GATOR!

ARRRGK!

THEN I CALL YOU PAPOOSE, AN' YOU CALL ME DUJOUR.

ALLONS, PAPOOSE, 'NESSA GONE. NOTHIN' IN THA WATER BUT DARK THANGS NOW.

THAT GLOWIN' LIGHT?

A SOUL, BO'. MY OLE LADY, TRAPPED 'TWEEN HELL AN' HERE.

MAN AIN'T EVEN HAD A DECENT MEAL!
YOU ALL RIGHT, MISTER?
STILL BREATHING, BO'.
THAT YO' HATCHET?
IT'S A TOMAHAWK CHARM, GIVE TO ME FROM MY GRAN'DADDY TO KEEP SAFE FROM SPIRITS.
'PRECIATE IT SAVIN' ME. YOU CAN SLANG IT, BO'! THROW IT LIKE A GENU-WINE PAPOOSE!
THAT'S CUZ I'M A FOR-REAL INDIAN! GRAN'DADDY SAID SO!

AN' I'M GONNA GET HER BACK.

WHERE YOU TAKIN' ME?
OWE YOU SOMETHIN', BO'. GOIN' TO PAY UP.
YOU CHANGED BACK THERE, RIGHT IN FRONT OF ME--
GOT A CURSE ON ME. CAN'T EAT NOTHIN' BUT WHAT DIES ON THE ROAD, AN' THE SPIRIT OF THEM I EAT FILL ME AN' CHANGE ME.
WHO HEXED YOU, DUJOUR?
"SHE MAGIC QUIZ INT'A TRAITOR, AN' HE BUSHWHACK HOOLIE AN' SKUNK--
"AN' HER OLE HOLLA MAN, CRAWDADDY, DROP CUZ--"

MAMA HOUDOO GOT ME. JUS' LIKE SHE HEX THEM SALA-MEN, FEEDIN' GATORS CURSED FLESH'A HER ENEMIES.
HER AN' THEM GATORBAIT BOYS GOT US ALL.
--AN' PULL BOUDREAU'S WANDER-SOUL RIGHT THROUGH HIS FACE.
MAMA HOUDOO SAVE FAMILY FO' LAST. CRUSH UP PAW AN' KID HER OWN SELF.

BUT YOU GOT AWAY?
SHE LEAVE ME TA SUFFER. DEAD FAMILY. DEAD CLUB. DEAD EATIN'.
PICK ONE. YOU DRAFTED, BO'.
CURSE'A EATIN' ROT AIN'T BAD ENOUGH? HE GOTTA TRY MAMA AGAIN?
DUJOUR AFTER NEW BLOOD, EH?

GOTTA GET 'TESSA BACK, PAPOOSE.
GOTTA CHANGE FAMILY CURSE MY CURSE.
BUT I NEED HELP. NEED MY CLUB.
YOU ROADKILL NOW.
Y'ALL STOP'IM, DADDY, HEAR?
RECKON OTHERS'LL JOIN UP?
THERE ARE OTHERS. DUJOUR MUST NOT REACH THEM.
CAN'T KILL'IM, NOW CAN WE? HOW WILL HE SUFFER IF HE'S RESTING?
DUJOUR AIN'T GONE QUIT, MAMA. NOT TIL HE'S DOORNAIL-DEAD.
CAN HE RIGHTLY HURT ABSENT A BREATH IN HIS BODY?

ANY CHOICE BUT TO KILL THE ONES DUJOUR FOUND AND CULL THE ONES HE'S 'BOUT TO?
HOW WE GONE FIND THE ONES HE AIN'T EVEN GOT YET?
THERE ARE WAYS TO SEE WHAT AND WHEN THE EYES CANNOT.
TIME FOR A HOOTENANNY, DADDY?
THEY BUT AWAIT YOUR RELEASE.

IS SCRYING TIME SO DIFF'ENT FROM SPYING DUJOUR IN HIS OLE MIRROR?
DOES PO' ALPHONSE NEED TWO EYEBALLS TO PLEASE MAMA? AIN'T ONE 'NOUGH?
YUH-YEAH, MAMA.
WHO?
WHO ARE THE ONES WHO WILL COME AGAINST GATORBAIT?
HOO!
HOO!
WHO SUCKLES BLOOD OF BABE AND BIRTHER?
WHO NESTS AT CROSSROADS OF TWO MINDS JOINED?
WHO SEES THROUGH NIGHT AND SHADE OF LIGHTLESS TIME?

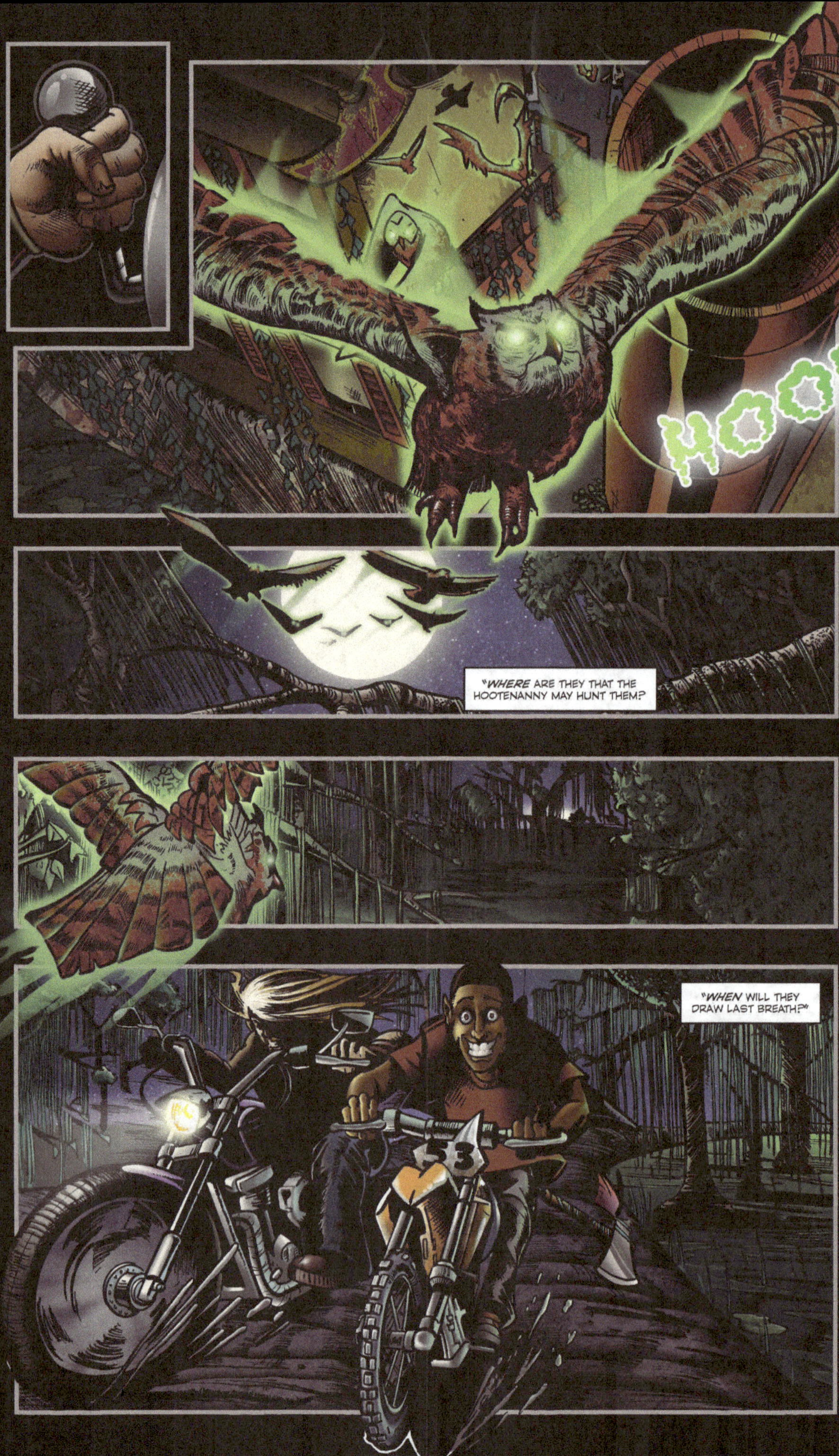

HOO
"WHERE ARE THEY THAT THE HOOTENANNY MAY HUNT THEM?
"WHEN WILL THEY DRAW LAST BREATH?"

"BROTHERHOOD AIN'T BIRTHED IN THE BLOOD.
"REAL BROTHERS IS THEM RIDE 'SIDE YA...

Ambulance

Transcon Medi-Vac
"...STAND 'SIDE YA IN A THROWDOWN...

"...TAKE YA IN WHEN AIN'T NOWHERE ELSE TA GET."

HOO!
"REAL BROTHERS...
"...THEY ONLY LEAVE YA WHEN AIN'T A BREATH LEFT TA BREATHE."

A TWO'FER, ROY! OLE' BUZZARD WAS GETTIN' HIS EAT ON!

AND NOW WE GONE GET OURS!

HIT THAT SY-REEN AND GET TO THE DINER!

TWO OP'EM!

LOOKS LIKE SECONDS FOR YOU, DUJOUR!
M'ONGRY, PAPOOSE, BUT CAN'T EAT BUT ONE CRITTER AT A SETTIN'. THAT'S THE CURSE.

JUST USE OLE SNAPPER FOR BAIT...

AH!
UH--
HAW!
...AN' OLE BUZZARD FOR WINGS!

GONE USE'EM TA FLY O'ER HERE AN' 'CRUIT SOME NEW BLOOD. EASIER WIT WINGS THAN WHEELS.
DON'T YOU LET NOBODY TOUCH MY BIKE, PAPOOSE!
AW, I GOTTA WAIT DOWN HERE BY MY LONESOME JUST 'CAUSE I AIN'T GOT WINGS?
MAYBE I'LL SMUSH MY OWN BIRD AND GOBBLE IT UP...
I SEE YA STILL HERE, BO'.
GET UP'ERE AN' SHOW SOME HOSP'TALITY.

'ERE WE GO! HOPE HE'S BITIN' TODAY!
SEND YA CRASHIN' BACK TA MAMA HOUBOO!
UNF! AIN'T COME TA HURT YA!
NEED YER HELP S'IL VOUS PLAIT!
OH, SHE SERVED MY INNARDS UP TA DIS FAT OLE CATFISH!
NOW, LISTEN! MAMA HOUDOO HEXED ME!

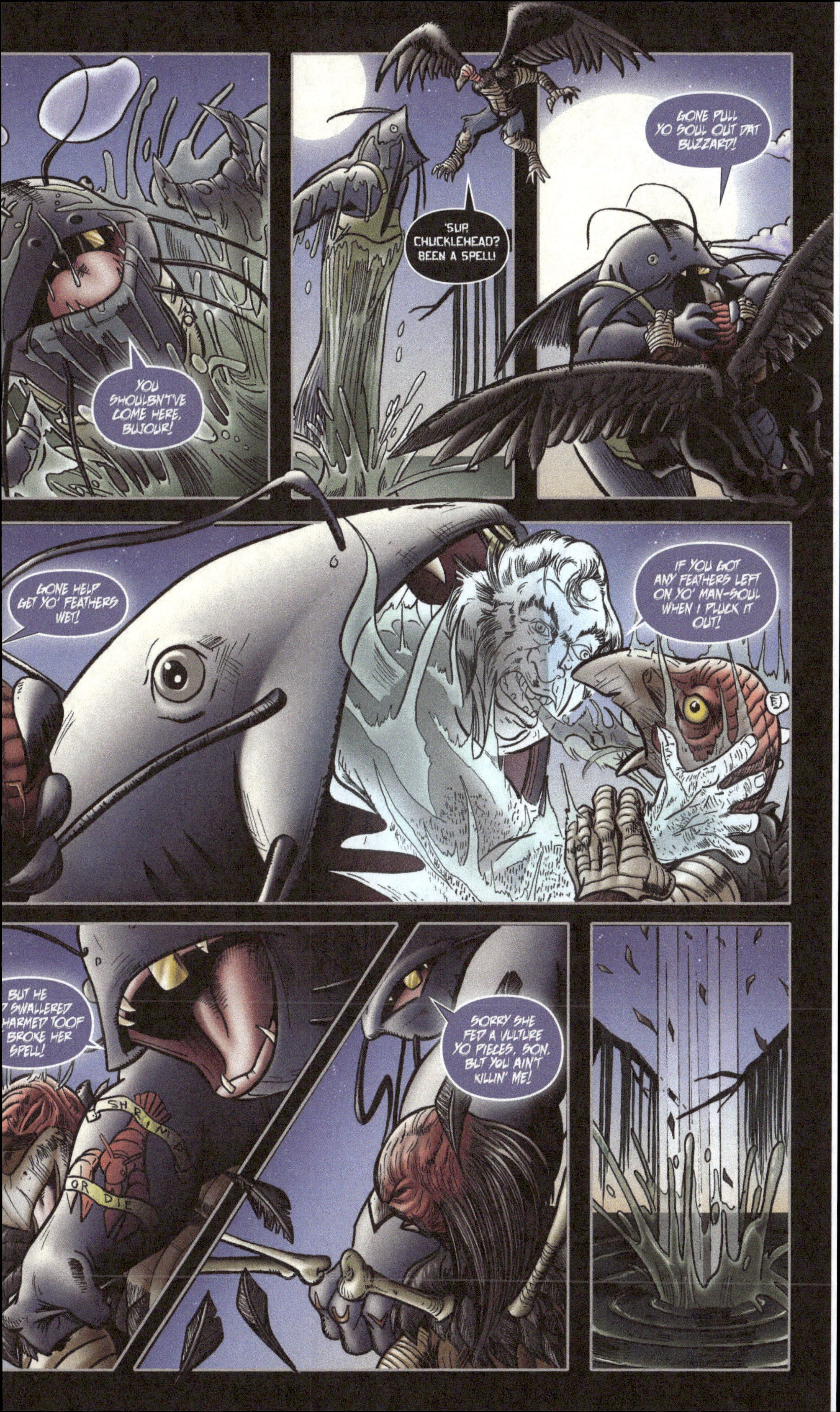

'SUP CHUCKLEHEAD? BEEN A SPELL!
GONE PULL YO SOUL OUT DAT BUZZARD!
YOU SHOULDN'T'VE COME HERE, BIJOU!
GONE HELP GET YO' FEATHERS WET!
IF YOU GOT ANY FEATHERS LEFT ON YO' MAN-SOUL WHEN I PLUCK IT OUT!

BUT HE SWALLERED HARMED TOO! BROKE HER SPELL!
SORRY SHE FED A VULTURE YO PIECES, SON, BUT YOU AIN'T KILLIN' ME!
SHRIMP OR DIE

WELL, I'LL BE! DAT BUZZARD DIDN'T EAT YOU...

GONE SQUARE DIS UP BY YOU.
JUS' SAY YA STILL GOT YER RIDE, CHUCKIE.

CHIMMIE'S PLACE.

YOU WANT SOME PLAY, SON?

...BUT I'M STAYIN' RETIRED!

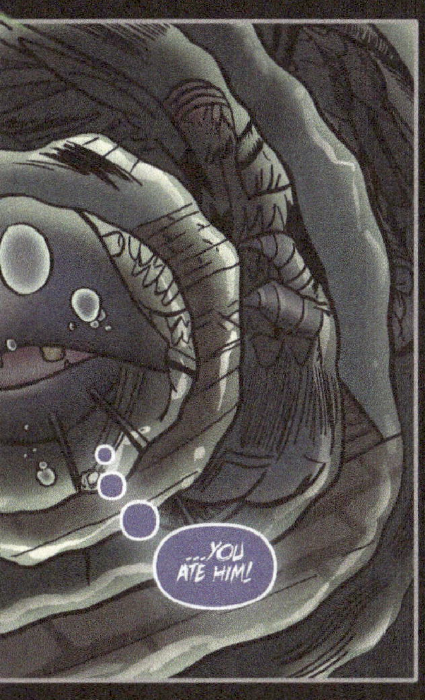
....YOU ATE HIM!

MY BAD, BIJOUR...

I SHO' FIGGERED MAMA HOUBOO FINALLY CUT YOU DOWN AN' MADE YOU ONE'A HER CRITTERS!

PLAY IF Y'ALL WANNA...

WHO'S WITH ME, BOYS?

WHO?

HOO!
HOO!
HOO!
HOO!
RETIRED, DAMN YA!
UHK--
CHUH-UH-CHUH!
EEE! EEE!

WHY Y'ALL AFTER ME?
I'M RETIRED.
HOO!
EE-YAGH!
MUH-UHM-MUH!
EEE! EEE!
CHIMMIE!
HAS CHIMMIE PASSED THE WAY OF THE HOOTENANNY?
ONE LESS TO ALIGN WITH DUJOUR, MAMA.

DARE I DREAM OF MINE ENEMY FINDING HIS HOPES HUSKS DRAINED OF BLOOD AND SPIRIT?

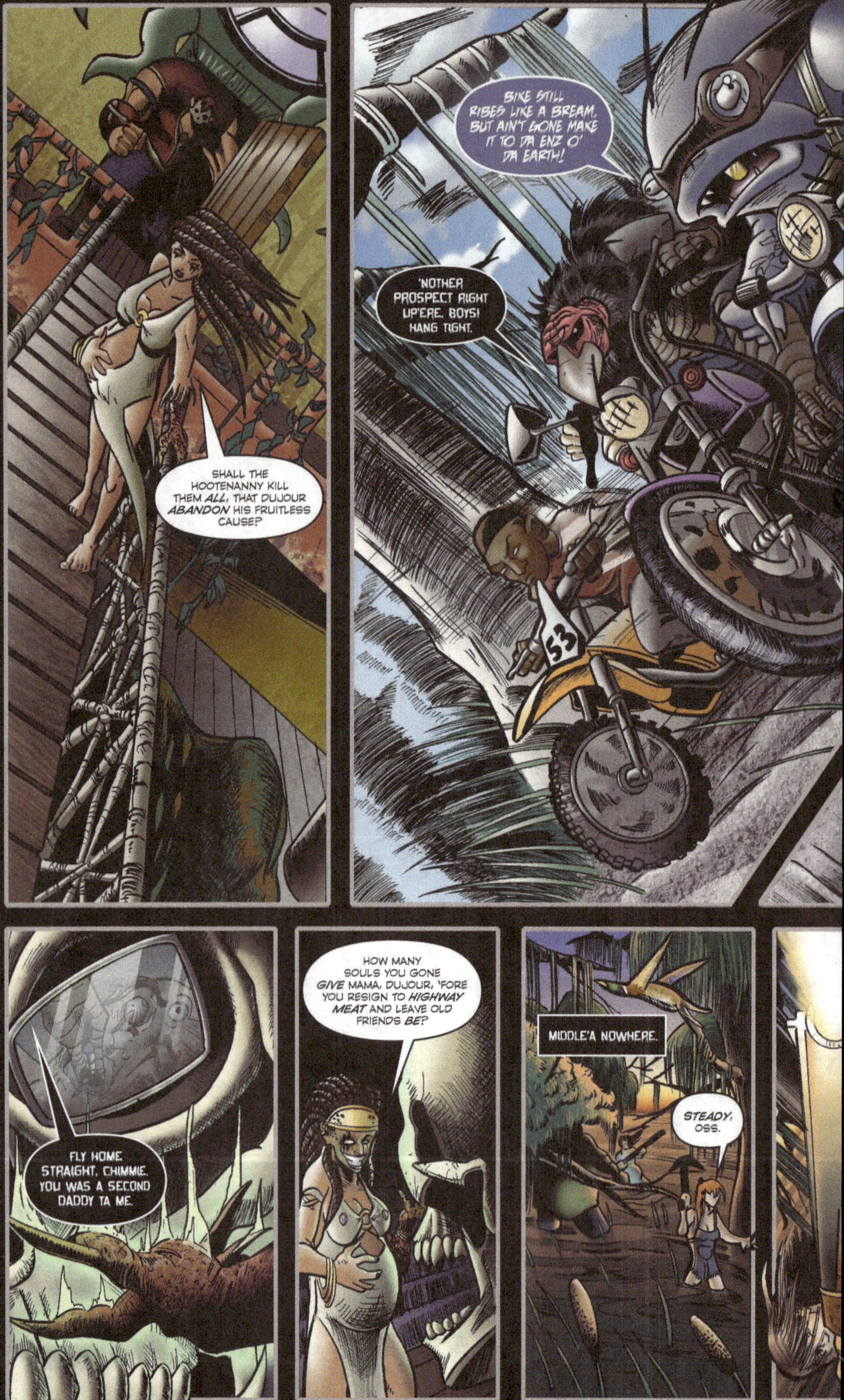

SHALL THE HOOTENANNY KILL THEM ALL, THAT DUJOUR ABANDON HIS FRUITLESS CAUSE?

BIKE STILL RIBES LIKE A DREAM, BUT AIN'T GONE MAKE IT TO DA ENZ O' DA EARTH!
'NOTHER PROSPECT RIGHT UP'ERE, BOYS! HANG TIGHT.

FLY HOME STRAIGHT, CHIMMIE. YOU WAS A SECOND DADDY TA ME.

HOW MANY SOULS YOU GONE GIVE MAMA, DUJOUR, 'FORE YOU RESIGN TO HIGHWAY MEAT AND LEAVE OLD FRIENDS BE?

MIDDLE'A NOWHERE.
STEADY, OSS.

DAMMIT.
S'OKAY, OSSIE.
GIRL, BOUDOIR EYES AIN'T FOR SHOOTIN'.

I GOT IT.
BIRD'S MORE SHOT THAN MEAT NOW, REARVIEW.

DON'T GLARE AT ME. I COULDA TAGGED IT IN ONE PULL!
WE'LL SEE 'BOUT THAT.

'EY, CHIMMIE!

WHAT THEY DONE TO YOU, OLE MAN?

THEY TOOK HIS LIGHT, DUJOUR! NUTHIN' LEFT.

BAD SIGN. NO ANSWERIN'...

THEM AIN'T DUCKS.
THEY COMIN' FOR MY BABY?
AIN'T NOBODY PULLIN' THAT BOY OUTTA YOU BUT ME, SUGAR.
MAMA HOUDOO'S SOUL-SLAVES!
400!
NOW, EAT UP WHAT'S INSIDE THAT HOOT-OWL!
SQUAAAH!
HOOOO
OSSIE, RUN!
CHAYA!
WHAT'S MAMA WANT WITH US?

HATE TO SPEND YOU, BUT YOU BEEN WASTIN' EVER' DAY SINCE WE PULLED YOU OUT MAMA'S SNAKE-MAN.
CHAYA, BABY, AIM TRUE.
CAN'T PUT THESE CRITTERS DOWN WITH METAL ROUNDS, CHAYA. GONE NEED YOUR SPECIAL SHOT TO CUT A PATH.
YOU KNOW WHAT THEM OWLS DO TO LADIES WITH CHILD, CHAYA!
I KNOW! GO! WHILE THEY PLUCK THE OUTSIDER!
GET SCARCE, GIRLS!
HOO!
ONLY SECONDS 'TIL THEY REND THE CORRUPTED.
THEN, THEY BACK ONTA US!
HOO!
HOO!
HOO!
CHAYA, NO! TAKE ME!

'POLOGIES, CHAYA. AIN'T YO' TROUBLES.
DUJOUR? SPARE THE LAMENTATIONS AN' TURN ME TO SHOOT!
AIN'T NO SHOOTIN' THE HOOTENANNY, GIRL!
NEED SOMETHIN' A LIL' MO' SPECIAL!
YOU DEAD, SON.
SKOMP!

FALSE TEETH?
TOY HATCHETS?
WHAT OTHER MAJESTIC CHARMS CAN YOU DIVINE TO CONFOUND MAMA, DUJOUR?
WILL TRINKETS HELP WHEN MAMA CALLS YOU FROM THE FIGHT?
WHERE'S MICKEY!?!
YOU STILL WANT THAT DISREPUTABLE CRITTER FOR A HUSBAND?
WHY DON'T YOU WED A MAN OF STATUS 'ROUND THESE PARTS?
DuJour
WILL YOU SACRIFICE YOUR LIFE WITH MICKEY FOR HIS LIFE WITHOUT YOU?
YES...
WILL YOU TAKE DUJOUR TO BE YOUR LAWFUL-WEDDED HUSBAND?

AIIRRGGGHH!

WHERE SHALL SHE HONEYMOON, CRAWDADDY?

STOP THAT SPOOK-LIGHT!
SHINY BALL!
BULLETS AIN'T WORTH NUTHIN' ON VAPOR!
GIVE ME A SHOT!
'NESSA, COME BACK!
THAT'S NOT YO' WIFE, DUJOUR.

HOO!
HOO!
CHAYA?

DON'T LET'EM TAKE MY BABY!
CAN'T LET'EM STEAL HER, REARVIEW.
GUNS AIN'T NO GOOD 'GAINST DEM BIRDS.
SHOOTIN'EM WILL JUST MAKE'EM DROP HER ANYWAYS, AN' WITH NO DUJOUR TO CATCH HER.

TROUBLE BREWIN' OVER HERE!
DUJOUR?
OH BOY, YOU AGAIN!
DUJOUR. I NEED YOU!
'NESSA!?!
MAMA GOT YOU WITH A HAINT, DUJOUR! WAKE UP!

DON'T LET THEM TAKE ME BACK, BABY!
I MISS YOU SO MUCH.
DON'T YOU DROP--
--ME!

THEN, WE GONE GO CATCH HIM.

DUJOUR! LORD KNOWS WHAT SNARE THAT SPECTRE LED YOU TO THIS TIME...

WHAT YOU DONE TO YO'SELF, DUJOUR?
WHY CAN'T I CATCH YOU, 'NESSA? EVEN WIT' WINGS LIKE LIGHTNIN', I CAN'T GET HOLD'A YOU!
BROKE THE OUT-HERE LIKE 'NESSA BROKE THE IN-THERE, BO'! YO' TOMMY-HAWK KILLS SOUL-THIEVES LIKE ME!
PUT IT TO ME!
AIN'T MY PLACE TO PUT YA DOWN. WE RIDE TOGETHER NOW.
LIKE A TRIBE, US AN' CHUCKLEHEAD AND THESE YOU JUS' BRUNG US TO.
AW, PAPOOSE, THEY AIN'T RIDIN' WIT' ROADKILL NOW.
I CUT AN' RUN FOR 'NESSA, LEFT'EM TO THE HOOT-OWLS.
OH, WE'RE RIDIN', DUJOUR. YOUR LEATHER IS OUR LEATHER, 'LEAST TIL WE FIND OSSIE AND GIVE MAMA HOUDOO WHAT SHE GETS.

WRONG
WAY

"BEST WATCH WHAT GOES IN YO' BELLY, BO'.
"NOT EVER'THANG LOOKS SWEET B'LONGS INSIDE YA."

"SOME CRITTERS GROW YA UP BIG, LIKE WHAT THEY SHOULD.

"OTHER'NS...

"...THEY JUS' FESTER IN YO' GULLET...

"...AN' ROT YO' INSIDES OUT."

HOPE YOU HUNGRY, DUJOUR!

PAPOOSE, YOU KNOW I DON' LIKE EATIN' NO SNAKE!
BEGGARS CAN'T BE CHOOSERS, SON. EAT DAT LOTIONMOUF OR I WILL!

--BUT AIN'T LIKE HE GOT A CHOICE.
YEAH, MAMA HOUDOO SPELLED 'IM. WE KNOW.
SOMETIME, THAT CURSE'S A BLESSIN', THOUGH.

I MIGHT HAVE'TA DINE ON SERPENT DU TREADMARK...

AIN'T NO SECOND CHANCES FOR THAT'UN, FULL'A MOCCASIN VENOM AS HE IS.

I'M GONE EAT IT, CHUCKLEHEAD. JUS' AIN'T MY IDEAR'A GOURMET STREET MEAT.
HE REALLY EATS THE ROAD'S DEAD, DON'T HE, REARVIEW?
THAT HE DO, CHAYA--
...BUT I BE DAMNED IF'N I'M GONE PICK RAT HAIR OUT MY FANGS AFTER SUPPA!
THAT MEANS YOU GET A SECON' CHANCE, BO'! RUN!
JUS' LIKE MAMA GONE BE WHEN WE RESCUE OUR LADY-LOVES!

YOU THINK IT SO SIMPLE, DUJOUR?

DOES HE RECKON TO STORM MAMA'S HOUSE HEAD-ON LIKE SOME EYE-GONE BULL, CRAWDADDY?

VENGEANCE IS BLIND, MAMA, AND LOYALTY DEAF ON TOP.

THEY'RE COMIN' FOR ME! CHAYA WON'T LEAVE ME TA YO' MERCY, HAG!

YOU THINK LOVE GONE STOP BULLETS AN' BLADES AN' BLACK WAYS?

WHAT'S LOVE GOOD FOR BUT KEEPIN' YO BABY BELLY BEIN' HOLLERED INTA HOOTENANNY NEST?

IS IT LOVE BRINGS ROADKILL TO MAMA'S DOOR, LIL' OSSIE?
HN!

YOU THINK LOVE GONE SAVE YO' TOMBOY FROM MAMA'S BOYS?

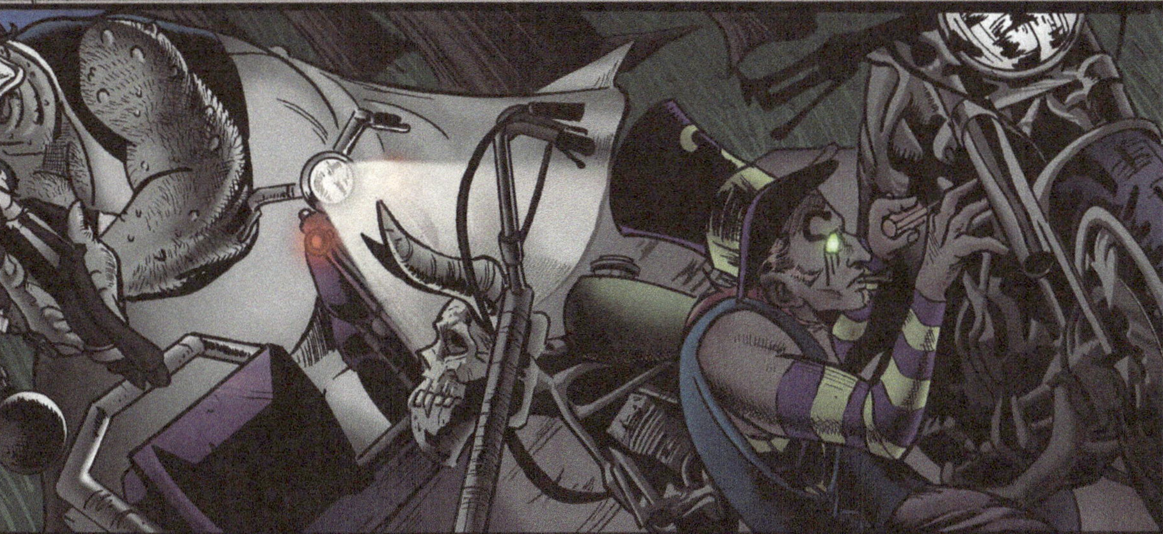

WON'T OSSIE'S SWEET LOVE BIND HER FAST TO OLE' LONESOME DUJOUR, CRAWDADDY?
FORGIVE ME, CHAYA...
NO! YOU CAN'T!

SHE'LL CUT A FINE SHAPE IN DUJOUR'S RING, MAMA. THEIR WEDDING CANDLE BURNS THE CEREMONIAL FIRES WHILE I HUNT ROADKILL.

WE JUST GONE ROLL THE SWAMPS 'TIL WE RUN 'CROSS DUJOUR AN' HIS TENDERFEETS, DADDY?

THE DRESS STINKS OF THAT GIRL'S AMOUR RIDING WITH ROADKILL, MUDPUPPY. ROUX-GA-ROUX CAN TRAIL THE ODOR RIGHT TO HER.

GRF!

Y'ALL LEAD. WE FOLLOW ON THE OLD RIVER ROAD.

QUIZ!

LIL' WOMAN AND BRIDEGROOM!

HIGHBEAM!

GATORBAIT, RAISE HELL!

SHOULD WE SPY OUR HUSBANDS GONE TA CLASH IN THE BAYOU, OSSIE?

SHALL YOU LOOK 'PON YOUR BETROTHED ONE LAST TIME A'FORE YOU TAKE THE VOWS?

YOU SURE YOU KNOW WHERE WE GOIN', DUJOUR?

A PLACE I AIN'T NEVER WANNA GO AGAIN, BO'. MAMA LIVE JUS' DOWN THE RIVER, FAR 'NOUGH WE NEED'A HURRY!

ROADKILL, HAUL ASS!

I FEEL YOU CLOSE, OSSIE, MY GIRL. WAIT ON ME, PRETTY. PLEASE, WAIT.

I CALL SHOT ON THAT BACKSTABBER, DUJOUR, Y'ALL!
NO ONE TOUCHES DUJOUR WITH FIST OR FIREPOWER!
DO YOU FRET MAMA GONE LET GATORBAIT END YO' LOVE A'FORE IT STARTS?
CHAYA...
CHAYA? WILL DUJOUR YOU WED TO SPARE YO' HANDSOME CHAYA?
WE GONE. FIND 'NESSA, FIND OSSIE, AN' GET GONE 'FORE WE GET GOT!

DUJOUR LIVES! IN SICKNESS OR IN HEALTH, BUT BREATHIN'! HEAR THAT, SUGAR?

THEY CLOSE NOW, ROUX? LISTEN TA DADDY AN' LEAVE DUJOUR BE AN' RAVAGE THE REST! GONE PUT THE PO' BASTARD BACK ON THE BACKWAYS WITH HIS ROAD PIZZA!

HOWWW-OOOOOOO!

I DO.

KILL THE OTHERS! LEAVE HIM BE!

WE GONE KILL MAMA HOUDOO, DUJOUR?

MAMA HOUDOO GOT HER A HAINT-SWAIN, BO', A DEMON BEAU POW'RFUL TOUGH INNA FIGHT!

OR DIE TRYIN'!

AW, DYIN' AIN'T SO BAD.

WHA-BUH-FUDH?!
GIRL PICKED THE WRONG ROADKILL FOR A DUNKIN' BOOF! COVER 'IS BACK, CHAYA!
WHAT YOU SAY, SIS'?
CHUCKLEHEAD DOWN, DUJOUR! LOOKS LIKE MUDPUPPY'S GATORBOAT!
DO YOU, OSSIE, TAKE DUJOUR TO BE YOUR LAWFUL-WEDDED HUSBAND?

DUJOUR AND PAPOOSE PLUS US IS FIVE! THEM'S FAIR ODDS!
FINE, I'LL COME BACK AN' KILL THEM'S LEFT WHEN THEY FINISH Y'ALL.
BAD ODDS ON WHEELS WITHOUT ME!
I DO...

--NOT!
CHAYA, I'M COMING, BABY!
AN' ROADKILL DON'T WIPE OUT TA GATORBAIT!
YOU CANNOT SAVE THEM, DUJOUR!
HE JUST DID!

ONLY RIGHT YOU DIE TA SNAKE FANGS AN' FORK TONGUE, QUIZ!
THE VEST IS HARDLY WORTH THE DANGERS IT BRINGS, EH, YOUNG ONE?
NOW, LET'S US HANDLE THE REST'A YO' CREW!
ROADKILL DON'T SCARE, MISTER!
WELL, IF IT AIN'T MISSUS DUJOUR COME TO CALL!
CHAYA! DON'T FRET NO MORE, BABY! I'M HERE!
OSSIE! SUGAR--
WHAT'S MAMA DONE TO YOU?
PUT ME TO A CHOICE, AN' THE ONLY ONE WAS YOU!
DUJOUR AIN'T GOT NO WIFE! MAMA'S CURSE PUTS FACE TO SPOOK-LIGHT, BUT HE 'MEMBERS SOMETHING NEVER WAS!
YOU GO TELL'IM, GIRL. NOW. WE GONE SET THIS RIGHT, I SWEAR.

YOU DONE SCRADH MY BIKE, SON!

I SWEAR!
I RAISED HIM FROM A PUP, BITCH!
AN' PAYBACKS IS HELL!

IF YA'D FED'IM KIBBLES 'STEAD'A PEOPLE FOOD, HE'D STILL BE BREATHIN'!

YAH!
I DO!
OH, GOD, REARVIEW IS DEAD! HE'S DEAD!
BUT HE AIN'T RIDIN' OFF ALONE!
YOU KNOW YOU BETTER RUN, NOW YOU'RE FREE OF THAT MONSTER MAMA ARRANGED YOU MARRY!

JUST 'CAUSE YO' EQUIPMENT IS BIGGER...
GRUFF!
...DON'T MEAN IT DOES THE JOB BETTER!
ROUX?
HOW-OOOOOOOO!
CAN'T MAKE THAT VEILED THREAT OF A FACE ANY UGLIER!
MY GROOM MAY TAKE ISSUE WITH YOUR CRITIQUE, FOR BETTER OR FOR WORSE!
FORGIVE US, CHAYA.
CAN'T LEAVE THIS CHORE TO YOU...

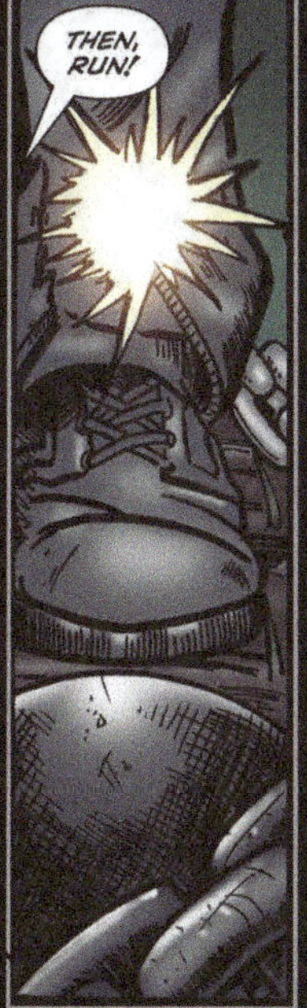

THEN, RUN!
DO!

COME AT ME, HAINT-SWAIN! YOU AIN'T NO BETTER'N TA KILL A BOY?
MAMA KEEPS YOU SPECIAL, DUJOUR! SHE ALWAYS SPARES YOU!
DUJOUR, YOU GOTTA LISTEN!
VANESSA!
I'M SO SORRY!
MAMA TOOK IT ALL!
AN' I'M TAKIN' SOME BACK! PAPOOSE, SLANG IT!
UNCAP THE VESSEL TO WHICH I WAS WED!
BUT I AM STILL OWED A SOUL UNFORSAKEN BY HER BRIDE!
CRAWDADDY'S DEMON INSIDE IS LOOSE!
WATCH OUT, PAPOOSE!

IT'S OSSIE...
DUJOUR. THERE AIN'T NO VANESSA. NEVER WAS. MAMA HOUDOO'S BEEN WITCHIN' BRIDES-TO-BE INTO SPOOK-LIGHTS LIKE ME TO CHARM YOU!
'NESSA?
NO 'NESSA?
I'M SORRY...
MAMA TOOK 'NESSA STRAIGHT OUT MY HEART, TOOK PAW AN' KID AN' THE GANG, TOOK RIGHT-FOOD FROM MY MOUTH...
THE THING WITHIN ME IS IMMORTAL! NO BLADE CAN--
--HUH--
BUT THIS IS MY GRANDADDY'S CHOPPER!
HUK--
HAAKKK!

YOU DOOMED HER WHEN YOU REFUSED TO ABANDON HER!
SHE IS MINE, NOW!
OSSIE, I LOVE YOU!
OH, PLEASE FORGIVE ME...

GET BACK!

THAT MOCCASIN CAN'T HOLD 'IM LIKE MY DADDY DID!
OLE' SNAKE FINALLY GETTIN' HIS EAT ON! CHEW DOWN, BO'!

BUT DON'T YOU FRET NO MORE, DADDY.
THAT THANG IS FINALLY GONE OUTTA YOU, AND YOU BEST BELIEVE I'M GONE GET ITS DEMON-SEED OUTTA MAMA NOW AN' STOP ALL THIS EVIL AN' LOSS!

EVEN IF I GOTTA PLEDGE ROADKILL TO GET IT DONE!

DEAD
END
STREET

"HUNGER CHANGE A BODY.
GO WITHOUT LONG 'NOUGH...

"...AN' B'COME
SOMETHIN' YA AIN'T.

"DO THANGS YA
OUGHT NOT..."

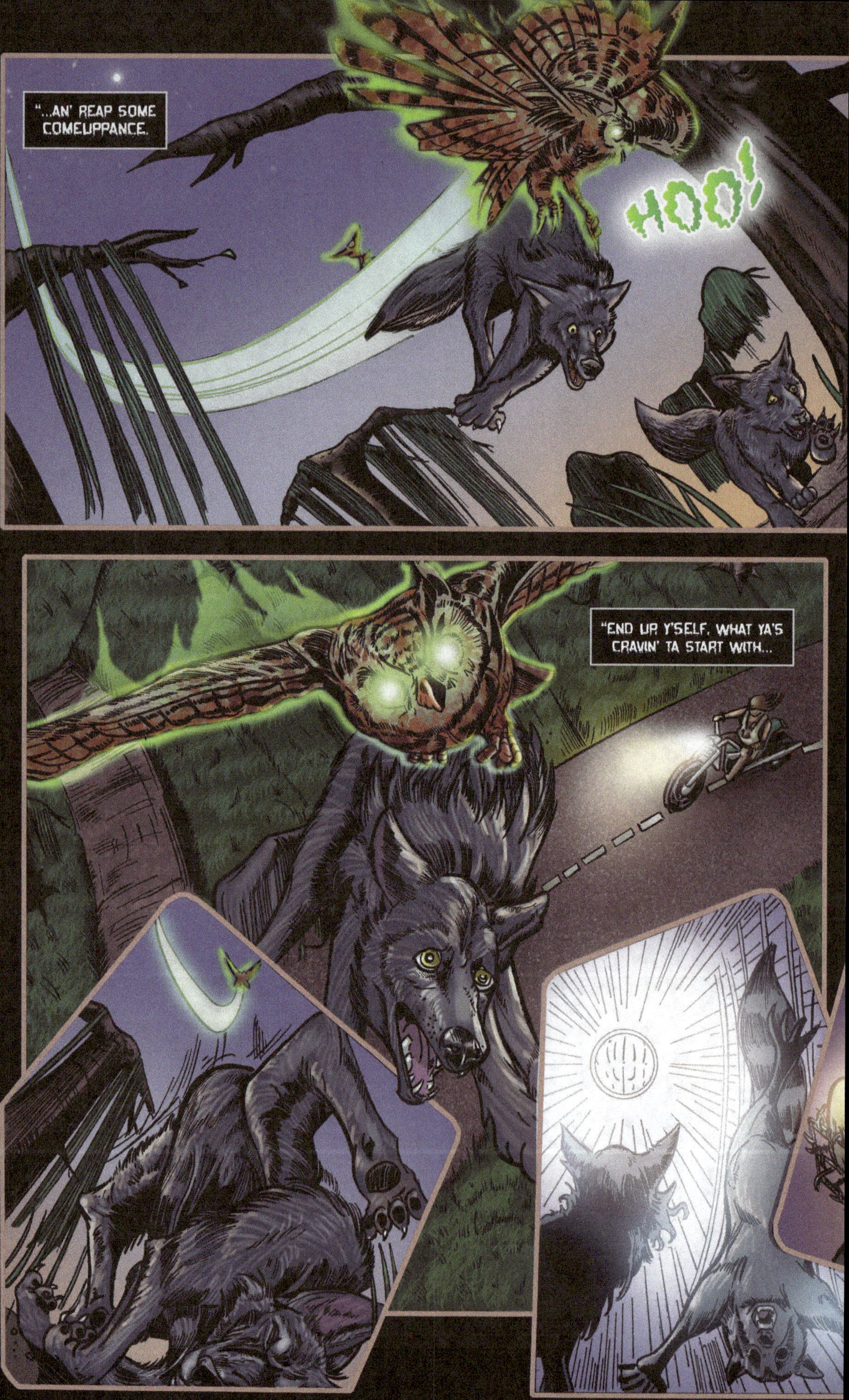

"...AN' REAP SOME COMEUPPANCE.

HOO!

"END UP Y'SELF, WHAT YA'S CRAVIN' TA START WITH...

HOW MANY MEALS CAN DUJOUR BYPASS ON THE ROAD TO MAMA'S HOUSE, MY HOOTENANNY?
WILL HE STILL HAVE APPETITE FOR MAMA'S NEW EGGS WHEN HE CALLS?
"...JUS' SOME OLE' MEAT ON BONE."

LOOK HERE, DUJOUR, YOU GOTTA EAT IF WE GONNA PUT MAMA HOUDOO DOWN, EVEN IF YOU JUS' ASSUME STANKY OLE' SKUNK KNACK!
AIN'T HAPPENIN', PAPOOSE. AIN'T EATIN' SINGLE 'NOTHER DEAD CRITTER FO' HER DAMN CURSE!
EVER' TIME I CHEW ONE DOWN, SHE VEX ME WIT' THAT 'NESSA SPOOK-LIGHT!
BETTER EAT SOMETHIN', DUJOUR! YOU DON'T LOOK SO GOOD.
AIN'T AVENGIN' MY BROTHER AND MY LADY WITH JUMPIN' LEGS AND A TONGUE BUILT FOR SKEETERS!
TELLYA... NO MO'... ROADKILL IN ...MY BELLY...

DOES DUJOUR REMEMBER THE TRUE CURSE, PETS?

MAYBE WE JUST NEED TA GO ON AN' FEED'IM A CRITTER, CHUCKLEHEAD?
MAN'S GOTTA RIGHT TA EAT WHAT HE WANTS OR DON'T WANT, SON.

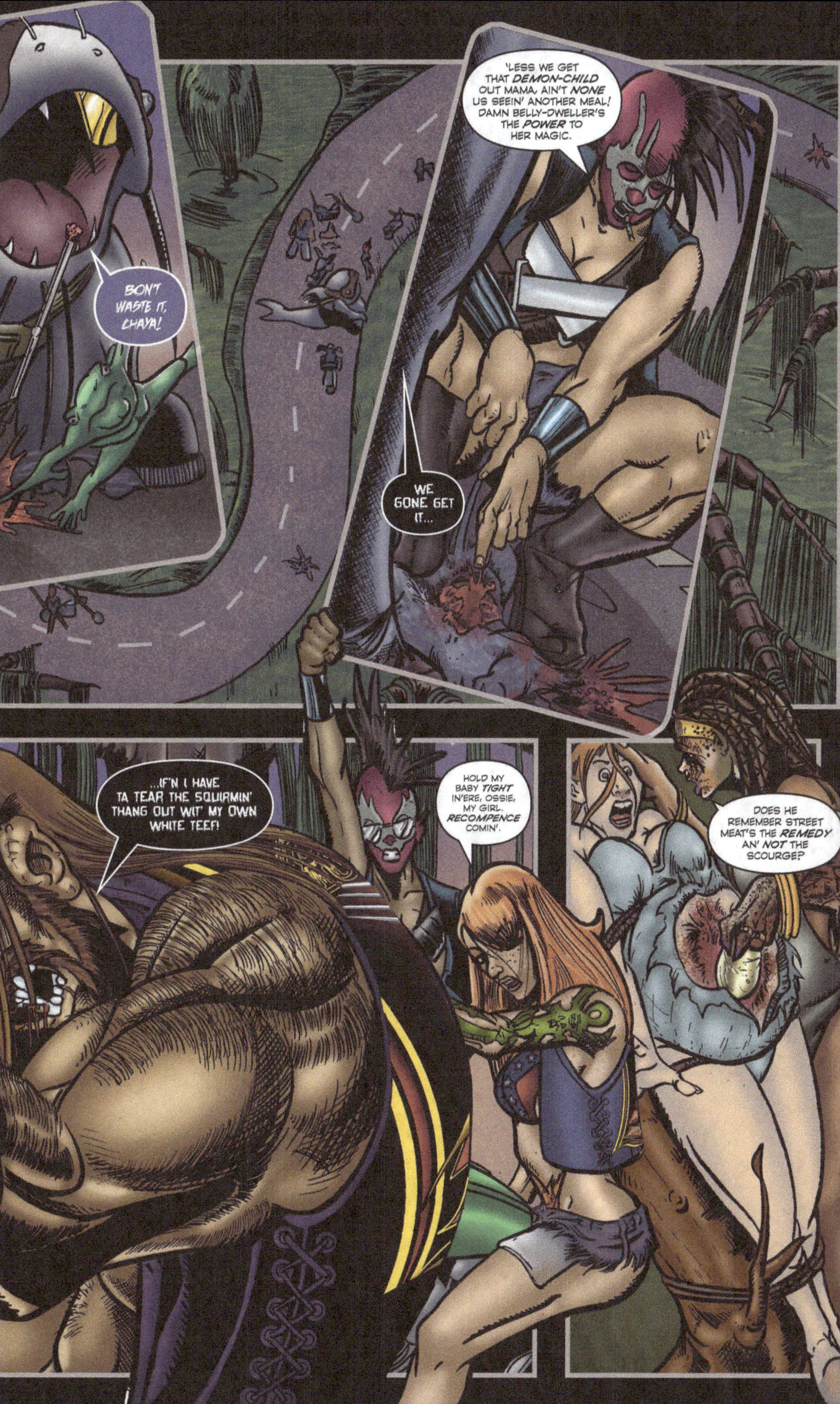

DON'T WASTE IT, CHAYA!
'LESS WE GET THAT DEMON-CHILD OUT MAMA, AIN'T NONE US SEEIN' ANOTHER MEAL! DAMN BELLY-DWELLER'S THE POWER TO HER MAGIC.
WE GONE GET IT...
...IF'N I HAVE TA TEAR THE SQUIRMIN' THANG OUT WIT' MY OWN WHITE TEEF!
HOLD MY BABY TIGHT IN'ERE, OSSIE, MY GIRL. RECOMPENCE COMIN'.
DOES HE REMEMBER STREET MEAT'S THE REMEDY AN' NOT THE SCOURGE?

SHALL WE REMIND HIM?

STOMACH'S RUMBLIN' FIERCE! LET'S RIDE!
HOO

DOES DUJOUR REALIZE SWALLOWIN' THE FOUL AN' THE ROT'S ALL KEEPS US FULL?

HOO!
'AY! HOOBANANNY!
GOTCHU BLEEDIN', CHUCKIE... SMELL IT...
GOT ALL Y'ALL BEAT UP AN' BLEEDIN', PAW...BUT WE WON, DID'N WE...
I 'MEMBER NOW... MAMA'S GATORBAIT DID'N TAKE US DOWN. SHE HAD 'NOTHER'N...A RINGER...
IT WAS ME!
I ATE ALL'A MY ROADKILL GANG!
ALL THAT PREVENTS US DEVOURIN' THE SACRED THINGS WE CRAVE TRUE AN' CAN'T ABIDE LOSIN'?

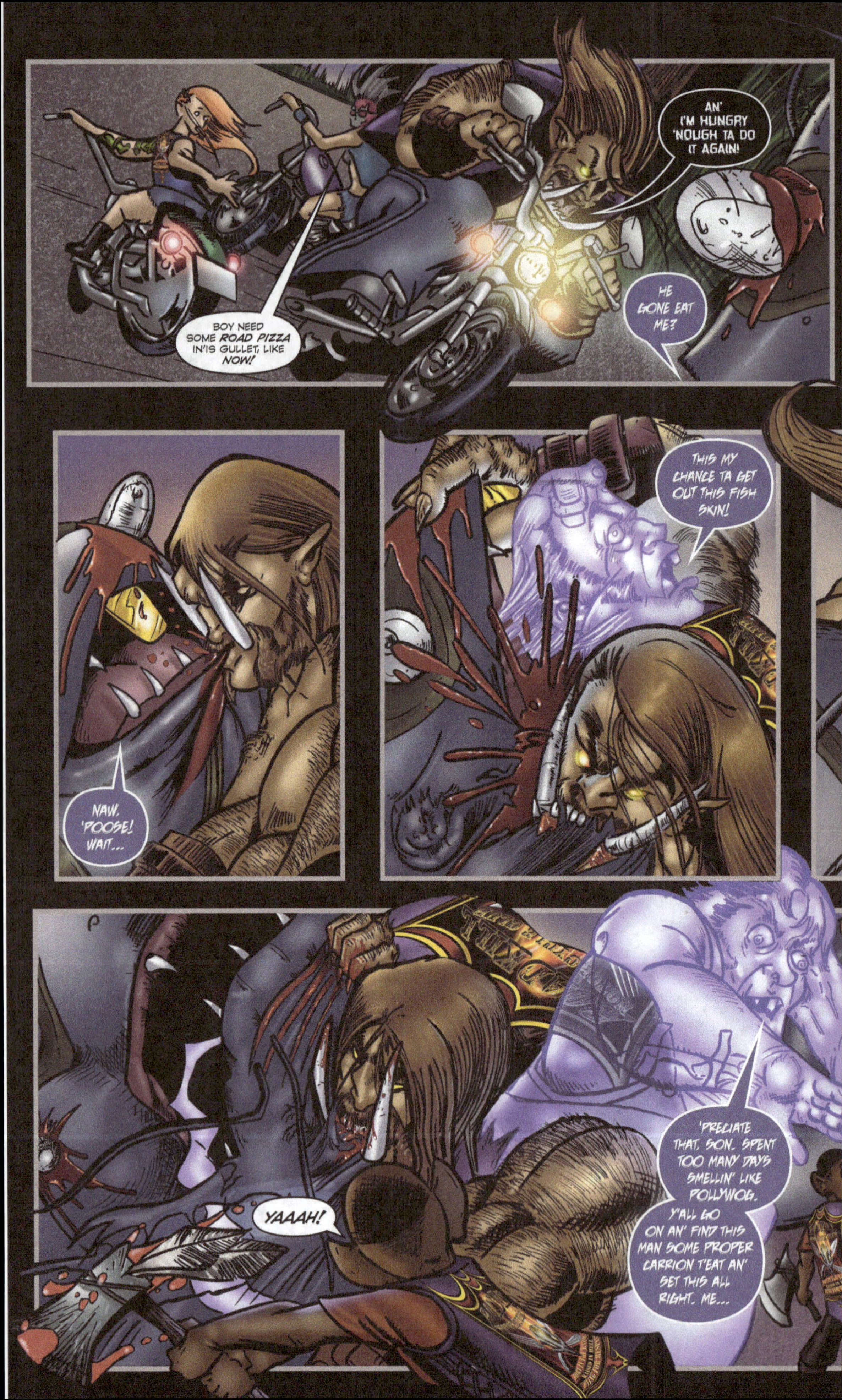

AN' I'M HUNGRY 'NOUGH TA DO IT AGAIN!
HE GONE EAT ME?
BOY NEED SOME ROAD PIZZA IN'IS GULLET, LIKE NOW!
THIS MY CHANCE TA GET OUT THIS FISH SKIN!
NAW, 'POOSE! WAIT...
YAAAH!
'PRECIATE THAT, SON. SPENT TOO MANY DAYS SMELLIN' LIKE POLLYWOG. Y'ALL GO ON AN' FIND THIS MAN SOME PROPER CARRION T'EAT AN' SET THIS ALL RIGHT. ME...

HYAAAAAA!
GONE EAT MY SOUL, BUJOUR?
BUT NOT ANY OLE' CHEAP MEAT...
HOOTERS ON TH' MENU! GET'EM!
DUJOUR, LET'IM UP!
WOO!
SON, I SAID FILET THIS FISH 'FORE HE EATS IT ALL UP AN' SNARES ME IN HIM FOREVER!
CUT ME, PAPOOSE! YO' CHARM'LL LET ME GO FROM MAMA'S BODY-CURSE!
BUT DUJOUR'S EATIN' YOU!
...I'M GOIN' FISHIN'!
NOM!
CATCH'EM ALL, CHUCKIE.

HOO!
HOO!
"GODDAMMIT! BOLTS ALONE AIN'T BRINGIN'EM DOWN!"
AN' I GOT NO SPARE SOUL-MAGIC TO TANGLE WITH TH'HOOTENANNY THIS TIME!
BUT DON'T YOU...
HOO?
AN' WE LOVE YOU.
ALWAYS.
FRE
FOREVER.
AN' EVER.

NO, I CAN'T... OSSIE...
YOU MUST, CHAYA. WE CAN'T STAY IN HERE FOREVER. HEAVEN AWAITS.
SEND US TO SAVE YOU.
I LOVE YOU BOTH.
AN' FOREVER!
YAAGH!
SUPPER'S READY!

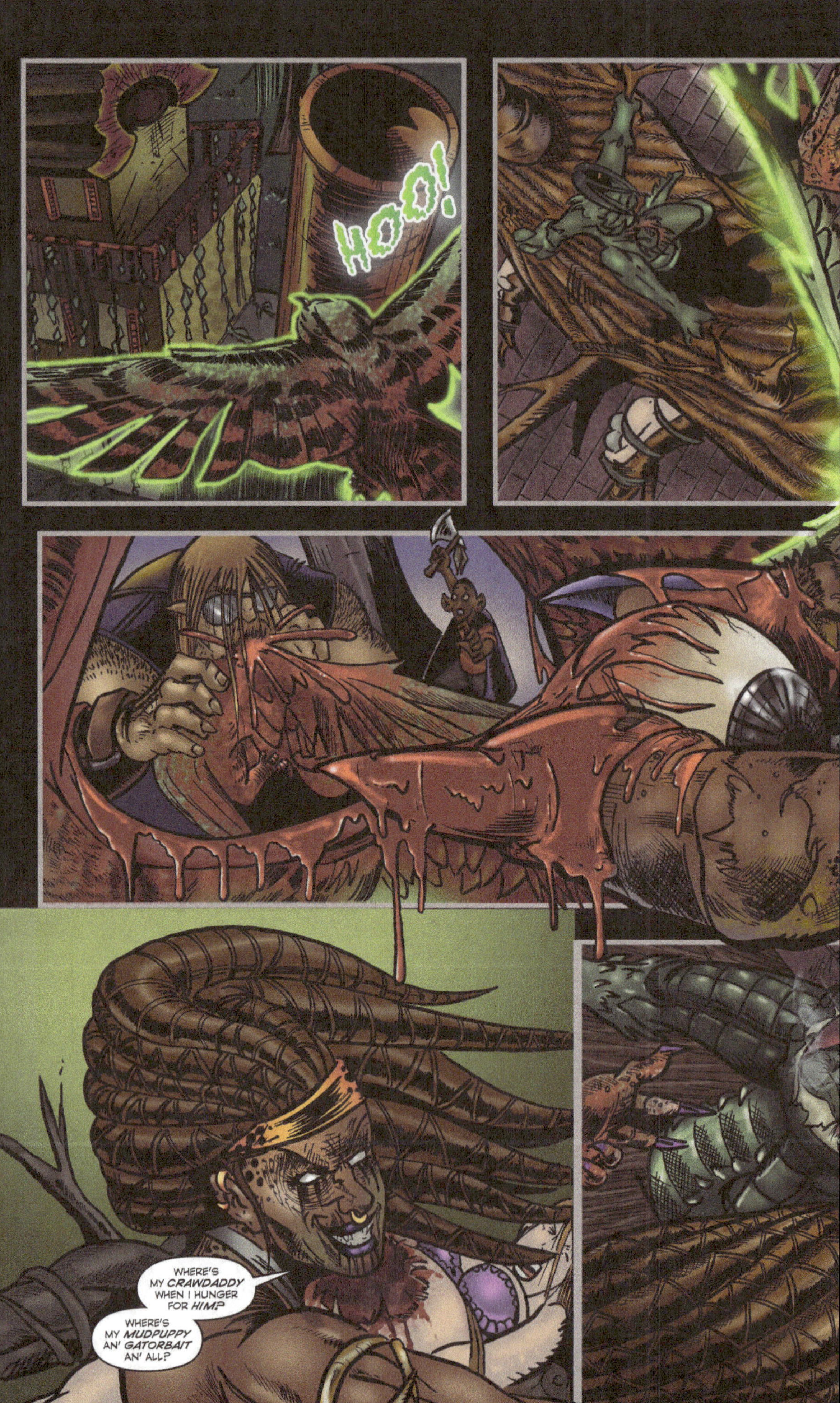
HOO!
WHERE'S MY CRAWDADDY WHEN I HUNGER FOR HIM?
WHERE'S MY MUDPUPPY AN' GATORBAIT AN' ALL?

WHO TOOK DOWN YO' BROTHER?

YOU RETURN ALL BY YOUR LONESOME, PET? YOU THE LAST ONE?

DUJOUR GIVE IN TO HIS HUNGER, EH?

BUT DON'T WE ALL?

YOU AIN'T GONE NEED NOBODY NOW, MAMA!

AIN'T DUJOUR TOOK'EM ALL FROM ME?

DOES MAMA EVEN NEED'EM ANYMORE, MY LITTLE ONES?

GONE LEAVE YOU WHAT YOU DONE LEFT ME!
HOO!
FEED!
US!
"WHO? YOU MEAN MAMA'S NEW BABIES? AIN'T THEY YO' NEW FRIENDS?"

NOTHIN'!
NOTHIN'? AIN'T HOT MEALS AN' NEW FRIENDS SOMETHIN'?
HOO-O!
KH!
ROADKILL'S HERE!
AN' MY HOOT-OWL SPIRIT COMIN' BACK ON ME!

I AIN'T GONE A DAY, MAMA, AN' YOU ALREADY ADOPTIN'!
NOW, WHO THESE HATE-BABIES COME FROM?!?
HOO!
HOO!
uhk...

Y'ALL TAKIN' ALL MY BABIES?
WHO MADE THAT BEAST INSIDE YOU NOW?!?!?
PLEASE DON'T TAKE HIM...
WHO'S THE BIRTHDAY BO'?
I AM BIRTHED FROM NO FLESH!
FOR I SPAWN FROM THE LOSS AT THE OTHER EDGE OF THE LIFESPAN!

I AM THE AFTERBIRTH OF THE SOUL'S SWEET RELEASE, THE UNGOTTEN, TWIN OF THE STILLBORN!
AIN'T YOU A ELOQUENT MORSEL...
GLUUK...
YOU TOOK IT EVER' BIT FROM ME, MAMA!
FAM'LY, PRIDE AN' A LOVE I NE'ER EVEN HAD!
WON'T YOU PUT HIM BACK IN ME, DUJOUR?

THE FISHTOOTH!
...JUS' FOR THE BITIN'!
...ALL FULL'A POWER MACABRE.
AN' ME WITH A BRAND NEW, GOLD TOOF...
NOW'S HIGH TIME TA REVERSE THAT CURSE, AN' TAKE SOME THANGS FROM YOU!
AAIIIEEE!

WHAT'D YOU DO, DUJOUR?
GOT Y'ALL VENGEANCE, HE DID.
AIGHH!
PUT... THE CURSE... TA HER...
MAMA KNOW NOW...
"ROADKILL LIVES AGAIN, AN' AIN'T NEVER GONE KNOW PEACE...
"...NOT 'TIL THEY EAT HER!"
END OF THE ROAD.

STOP

SHAWN HARBIN
GM 2014

Art by Laura Guzzo

www.ingramcontent.com/pod-product-compliance
Lightning Source LLC
Chambersburg PA
CBHW081920130726
47909CB00015B/3058